Hotwife And The Boyfriend From The Past - A Wife Watching Hotwife Romance Novel

Hot Wife Shared

Karly Violet

Published by Karly Violet, 2020.

This is a work of fiction. Similarities to real people, places, or events are entirely coincidental.

HOTWIFE AND THE BOYFRIEND FROM THE PAST - A WIFE WATCHING HOTWIFE ROMANCE NOVEL

First edition. November 16, 2020.

Copyright © 2020 Karly Violet.

ISBN: 979-8201489397

Written by Karly Violet.

Hotwife And The Boyfriend From The Past

A Wife Watching Hotwife Romance Novel

Chapter One: A Surprising Find

"Denise is outside," my wife says to me as I stand at the kitchen sink. Our neighbor is a nice older woman who enjoys speaking to Tonya whenever she gets the chance. Today being Saturday, we are both home and we have just now made our way to the kitchen for some breakfast. The woman outside tends to be up and outside her house tending her garden well before we get up on the weekends.

"I wonder what she wants to tell you about another neighbor," I quip as I look at Tonya and smile.

She laughs. "Well, I suppose I should get out there and find out." My wife turns and walks to the front door to go outside. I watch through the kitchen window as the two women talk to each other.

"Gossiper," I chuckle to myself as I reach for a cup from the cabinet. The coffee maker is humming along and soon I will have a nice warm cup of java to help wake me this morning.

Tonya's cell phone buzzes on the countertop nearby. I look over and quickly read the notification. "Marcus?" I say to myself as I watch the screen dim and the notification disappear. "Who's that?" My wife and I both work at the same place, a company where I am the shipping manager and she is a retail sales specialist. We met there almost three years ago and have been married to each other the last two. Needless to say, I know almost everyone where I work as well as on Tonya's side of the building. The name *Marcus* is not one that I am familiar with.

Moving the phone around, I allow one quick look out through the kitchen window to make sure that Tonya is still occupied with Denise. Seeing that she is, I enter her passcode on the phone. I figured it out months ago while playing around with her phone and though I meant to play a prank on her to show her the importance of keeping her password difficult to guess, I have yet to do that. Using your wedding date is not exactly the best form of password security around.

After going into the text messenger on the phone, I find the message that has just come in as well as several others from the same person. "What are you wearing this morning?" he asks.

"Who the fuck are you?" I mutter under my breath as I scroll to one from earlier this morning.

"Tonya, I had a wet dream last night. You were great." My heart begins to race as I shake my head. I go back to the message before this one and read it. "You need to send me something more than just a few dirty words, baby. Let me see your tits."

"Her *tits?*" I look up and out the window of the kitchen. Tonya and Denise are laughing together as I try to understand what is going on in these messages. She is obviously reading them and has not told me that another man is harassing her. This must mean that this conversation is mutual. This assumption proves to be correct as I find a message from her to him a little earlier.

"Marcus, you are such a bad boy. You know I would love to let you fuck me hard, right? You could push my legs back and put my feet on your shoulders. It would feel so good." There are several heart and kissing emojis at the end of the message. My body begins to shake from the sudden realization that Tonya has been sexting some other man. Why the hell is she doing this?

The front door suddenly opens and I realize that my wife is coming back inside. I close the texts and lock her phone just as she closes the door. Tonya walks up to me and says, "Denise thinks someone is stealing her newspaper."

I try to clear the pained expression on my face as I turn toward her and reply, "Who still gets newspapers?"

"Exactly," she giggles before walking up to me and giving me a tight hug. "I think that woman is just looking to go after someone, though. It must be boring without her husband around." Denise's husband left her last year for another woman. A *much younger* woman. I get that such a thing would mess with someone's frame of mind, but right now I have a tough time feeling bad for our neighbor. Tonya has been sexting with some guy and possibly screwing him behind my back. How do I handle that? What do I say?

"You know, we don't talk about work much anymore," I say as I move the cup of coffee around in my hands. "How are things going for you on your end of the building?"

My wife raises an eyebrow as she chuckles. "We decided a long time ago to keep work at work, Russ. You know that."

"Yeah, I know, but I worry about you over there sometimes. I mean, who works in your office again?"

"You know who works in my office," Tonya replies with a strained look on her face.

"But tell me again. I think I might have forgotten their names."

My wife sighs. "Well, there's Sadie and Tommy just across the room from me. Then there's Justine. That's all the others in my immediate office. Why?"

I shrug my shoulders. "Didn't your office hire someone recently?"

Tonya shakes her head. "No, I don't think so. What's this all about, Russ?" Her blue eyes focus on me as I try to think of a way to figure out who the hell Marcus is.

"I don't know, honey. I must have dreamed it or something. Maybe it was that wet dream I had about you." I study her face as I use the same phrasing as her text message lover. If there is anything different in her expression, though, I cannot see it.

"You had a wet dream?" Tonya laughs as she reaches down and taps the growing bulge in my shorts. I suddenly realize that the thought of her talking dirty to some other man has made me horny as hell. Why would I be so horny over that sort of thing?

Swallowing hard, I put my coffee down and tell her, "You know that I have all sorts of wet dreams for you, my love. I would hope that you have them for me too."

Tonya smiles. "You know that I do, Russ. I always dream about you." She pulls my head down so that she can kiss me. Her soft, full lips press against mine as her tongue explores my mouth. My wife is a wonderful kisser and has always had a way of getting my mind focused on her and away from anything else. Maybe she is doing that now? Maybe she knows that I know about the other man and she wants to move me on from the subject of her written desires?

"You're fucking hot," I tell her as I back away and look into her eyes. "There are a lot of men who would do anything to get with you."

Tonya's face turns bright pink. "Russ, you are so full of yourself today, huh?"

"I'm serious," I reply. "Other men really like you. Haven't you found that men want to get you into bed?" Though she takes this as simply joking around, the importance of the question fills my mind. I want to know whether Tonya has had thoughts about other men and their lust for her.

"That's a really weird thing to ask. Russ, what are you up to?" My wife studies my face. She knows when I am prodding her for something.

"I know, but I just thought I would ask. There are lots of guys who talk about you at work and around town. You are the hottest woman around, Tonya. You can't blame me for thinking that there might be one or two of those guys who might approach you for something more than just friendship."

My wife smiles at me as she moves a hand up to my cheek. Caressing it, she tells me, "You shouldn't be so worried about that sort of thing, sweetheart. You know as well as I that I only have eyes for you. Sure, there are probably a few men who give me an extra look or two, but the same can be said about other women and you. There are ladies in this neighborhood who would try to seduce you if they had any chance at all. Take Denise, for example..."

"*Denise?*" I laugh hard as I think of the middle-aged woman. "There is no way that I would go for her."

"I know that, but it doesn't mean that she wouldn't like to have a turn with you, Russ. She's a woman who is still in her sexual prime, but she doesn't have anyone to share that with anymore. Maybe you should go over to her house and offer to give her a nice poke."

"Are you serious?" I laugh again as I think about my wife's use of the term *poke*. "Tonya, that's just not right."

"And you worry about other men around me? Sweetie, I'm yours and only yours." My wife steps closer to me once again and kisses me harder this time. She is trying to prove something to me as she pushes her tongue into my mouth for a second time. I enjoy the feeling of her lips on mine and the way she nips at me, but my mind is still caught on what the text messages on her phone said to her. Whoever this Marcus is, Tonya is not going to tell me about him very easily.

My wife pulls away from me and smiles as she touches the bulge in my shorts. She turns and walks toward the bedroom after picking up her cell phone. A chill runs down along my neck and back as I consider what she has been talking about in her text messages to the other man. Should I be worried? It could be a simple case of two people screwing around verbally, but I feel as if there could be more to this. Tonya is a highly sexual woman and it would not surprise me to find that she had found another man to help her with her needs.

"Dammit," I mumble quietly as I take another drink of my coffee. Setting the cup down for a second time, I decide to take a walk outside. I need to clear my mind and think about what I have seen on Tonya's phone. Whether I bring up the messages could depend on how I want the conversation to go. For one thing, my wife values privacy. She will be very upset when she discovers that I have gotten onto her phone and read her messages. There will be no way for me to explain that away. So, I will need to be certain as to whether I want to stir that soup or just leave it alone. A nice walk will help to clear my mind so that I can consider my options.

Chapter Two: Sorting it Out

The smell of the bar is somehow comforting as I sit down with my two old friends, Theo Davis and Adrian Whitaker. I have known the two men since elementary school and we have all three shared some of our deepest, darkest secrets with each other. Tonight, as I sip a little beer from a bottle, I decide to ask the two of them what I should do about what I have discovered.

Beginning to speak, I find myself not quite able to be completely honest with my friends. "There is this lady at work," I say as I put my bottle down on the table. "She works in another department and I have rarely spoken to her. A few days ago, she accidentally sent me a couple of emails that were meant for someone else; another man who works in my department at the company." I pause as I watch my two friends' expressions.

"And?" chuckled Adrian. "Isn't that something that happens at companies?" He smiles at me before taking another sip of his own adult beverage.

I nod my head. "Well, sure, people email each other all the time, but this wasn't really business-related, if you know what I mean."

Theo raises an eyebrow. "Some personal emails? The sort that could make someone blush?" I nod my head as I look over at him. "Well, shit. Were they good?" The two men laugh and I join in with them as my heart leaps into my throat. I want to tell them what I found on Tonya's phone, but then again I do not want them to know that my wife would do such a thing. At least, not yet.

"The woman, I'll call her Ann, asked the guy whether they were on for the weekend and if he wanted her to give him a blow job."

"Shit." Theo sits forward in his seat. "This is getting good."

"Did you answer her?" Adrian asks. He is still sitting back in his seat as if what I have said does little to surprise him.

"No, I didn't do that," I reply. "It would be really embarrassing if I were to do that."

"But, what's the problem, then? Two people using work email to set up a date to screw each other seems pretty typical," Adrian observes. "I mean, I do it all the time." My friend is an oddity of nature. He is able to convince practically any woman at any time that they should have sex with him. It does not matter that he is only five-six and not the most attractive man around. Adrian knows how to swoon the ladies. It is a skill that many of us who know him wishes he could teach us.

"She's married," I blurt out. "He isn't, but Ann is married."

"Oh, shit," Theo says while shaking his head. "Do you know the guy?"

"Yeah, I know him." Once again I wish I could just tell them what is really going on. I do not want to change the story at this point, though. Everything is set in motion. "But Ann's husband would not be happy."

"Dude, you need to shut that shit down," Theo replies. "Forward the emails to her husband and get this thing stopped. She shouldn't be cheating on her man."

"I'm worried about how her husband might react," I tell my friends. "He could end up being pretty cool about things, but he could also be the sort of guy who will be a real prick about things. Besides, if I tell him about the emails it might ruin an otherwise decent marriage."

"An *otherwise decent* marriage?" Adrian finally sits forward and puts his elbows on the table as he looks at me. "How is it a decent marriage if the wife is cheating on her husband?"

"I don't know. He's come around a couple of times for office parties and he seems like a nice guy. Honestly, I think he adores his wife." Of course, I am thinking about my own relationship with Tonya, but I do not want Theo and Adrian to know that. I love my wife and I think we do have a great marriage. Had I not found the messages, this conversation would not be happening right now.

"Tell him," Theo says as he shakes his head. "It's not fair to keep him in the dark like that. His wife is a bitch for doing that behind his back anyway. She deserves to get herself kicked out of the house and divorced."

"That's a little too much, don't you think?" Adrian chimes in as he looks at Theo. "Sure, there's something going on, but if the husband is fine with her the way she is, why make waves?" He turns his attention to me and adds, "Besides, that would mean that your ass is in the middle of it, Russ. I don't see you as the type of guy who wants to be in the middle of someone else's shit."

Nodding, I tell him, "I don't want to be in their shit, but she sent me the emails. I think Ann has already put me there."

"Just drop it," Adrian insists. "There will be no good that comes out of this. The two of them will end up in an argument and then in divorce court. You will then be asked to appear in court as a witness for the husband. It would be best to just leave this all alone, man. Don't get involved in something that has nothing to do with you." Unfortunately, it has everything to do with me, but I still don't want to tell the two men what has actually happened.

"Squeal her out, Russ," Theo advises. "If my wife was fucking around behind my back I would want to know about it. The guy has a right to know so that he can make his own decision. Drop it all off into his lap and move on. Do it anonymously."

"Anonymously? How the hell could I do that?"

"A new email account with a fake profile, brother. That's what I do whenever I email some asshole about something I don't like." Theo is the ultimate arguer when it comes to trying to get something straightened out in his life. It might have something to do with the very strong wife that he has and the way his life changed after he met and married her. Having been relatively bashful before, the man is now brazen in how he deals with other people.

"Maybe," I agree. "I'll look at that." A server walks over to our table and smiles at us.

"Would you guys like another round?"

Adrian smiles. "How about another round for us and a round for you and me after you get off work." Chill bumps rise along the back of my neck as I watch my friend work his magic.

"I don't know about that, honey. The management here doesn't like us to fraternize with the customers." Her brown eyes focus squarely on Adrian as he smiles at her.

"I don't plan to fraternize with you, sweetheart," he replies. "Just a nice walk and maybe an ice cream from that late night food trailer down the street. I'm a nice guy. I just want to have someone to hold a conversation with after these two go home."

The server looks at the two of us and then back at Adrian. "I'll think about it. Let me go get those drinks." She smiles before turning and disappearing, giving the three of us a nice look at her ass.

"Shit, man," Theo says with a chuckle as he looks over at Adrian. "I would never believe it if I didn't see it with my own eyes. You are a player."

"And a damned good one," Adrian replies with a laugh. "You two guys are tied down, but I am a free agent. It's time to get it on tonight."

I shake my head. "She agreed to some ice cream and a walk, Adrian. I don't think she is considering sex with you."

A wicked grin crosses his face. "She was thinking about sex with me before I even spoke to her. Otherwise, she would have blown me off completely when I asked her out. You guys should ditch your wives and learn from the master."

I laugh. "Theo and I found our women and we married them. I think that puts us one-up on you."

"Here you are," the server says to us as she returns with the beers. She then slips a small piece of paper beside Adrian's bottle. "I'm off at nine. You had better be a gentleman." She looks at our friend with a smirk before walking away.

"Holy shit, he's right. She's going to fuck his brains out," Theo says while shaking his head.

"She told him to be a gentleman," I reply. "That's not an invitation to sex."

"It certainly is," Adrian says with a smile still on his face. "You need to learn how to read women, Russ. Sometimes they do things to make a point. She was making a point. She expects to have sex with me tonight."

"No way."

"Then tell me, buddy; what are you going to do about that email problem?" Adrian's eyes stare hard into mine. "That's the big question for you now, right? You had better get that shit figured out soon because Ann, or whoever the lady is, will be riding dirty with that guy in your department. I say leave it alone, but I can see Theo's point too. If you do this, though, don't leave anything out. Tell him everything and leave it to him. Then you can just step back and watch the fireworks."

"He's right," Theo says while nodding his head. "You need to just put it all at the husband's feet and let him deal with it."

"But, what if it's just sexting by email? Would it be worth doing then? What if they haven't had sex yet and they don't really want to?"

"Dude, do you even hear yourself?" Theo responds to my question. "It never stops at that. Sexting, sexual emails, whatever it is, man; it won't stop until it stops."

I sigh. "That's tough to know."

"Not for you, right? Be glad you have a nice wife, Russ," Adrian says to me. "If you didn't have her and the pity she has for you, your life would suck right now." We all laugh, though I feel a little like I have just lost something inside. If Tonya is doing more than sexting this guy named Marcus, I'm not sure when or where it is happening. She has not been trying to get away from me for trips or other reasons. Of course, she could be leaving work sometimes without me noticing. That is especially possible because the entrance to her side of the building is opposite to mine.

"Let us know how it goes when you decide what you are going to do," Theo says before taking a sip of his new beer. Nodding my head, I pick up my first bottle and finish it down before going to the second one. There is so much for me to figure out soon that I do not know whether I want to face the facts. For some reason, Tonya has decided to share very explicit messages with another man. It could just be some semi-harmless fun, but it could also be something that could lead to the end of our marriage later. The decision as to whether I should confront her will have to wait for a day or two as I figure things out. Oh, how I wish I knew who Marcus is! That would at least help me answer whether their intentions are the sort that would put my marriage to Tonya in jeopardy.

Chapter Three: A Cute Guy

"I hope you girls are not going to get too drunk," Tonya says to her friends as they sit on the patio of a small Italian restaurant just on the edge of town.

Treena leans toward her after having some wine. "You know, I don't get to go out with the hubs much anymore. I don't go out unless it's with you and the girls. If I want to tie one on, I'm going to tie one on." She giggles and laughs before moving some of her blonde highlights over her ear. As I sit and think about Russ out with his guy friends at the bar, I wonder what they are talking about. Are they as silly as my friends when we have a little too much to drink?

"So, this guy," Sarah says with a wry smile on her face. "Is he cute?" I shoot a stare toward Laney.

"I'm sorry, Tonya. They pulled it out of me on the way over here. You know that I can't hide things from them." The youngest member of our little four-girl crew is often the easiest to get something out of. I should have kept from sharing what has been going on between me and Marcus.

"Don't blame her," Sarah says with a smile. "We're just curious, alright? No judgment here, girl. What's his name?"

Swallowing hard as I sit back in my seat, I tell her, "His name is Marcus."

"Wait, I know that name," Treena cuts in. Her eyes grow large as she looks over at me. "Sweetie, you are not talking about *the* Marcus, are you?"

"It's just some harmless text messaging," I reply as I look at the three of them. "It's not like I'm leaving Russ for him."

"Shit, you are a glutton for punishment," Treena says while shaking her head.

"What do you mean?" Laney asks.

Treena sits forward in her seat. "Marcus is an old boyfriend of hers, right, Tonya?" The women all sit and look at me until I become extremely uncomfortable with all the attention.

"Dammit, we are still friends."

"More than friends," Laney says quickly. She then sits back in her seat as she realizes that she has once again offered more information than she should have.

"Are you fucking him?" Sarah asks with great interest.

"I'm married, Sarah," I reply quickly. "There is only one guy I am having sex with at the moment." I look around at the other restaurant guests nearby on the patio. The street traffic appears to be drowning out what we are saying at our table.

"That doesn't matter. At least, not with Marcus," Treena offers. "If you are talking to him again, it means you are hot for him, Tonya. Fess up and tell us what you have going on." She eyes me hard as I look away. Now that the proverbial cat is out of the bag, I suppose there is nothing else to do but level with my friends.

"He's an ex, that's true, but we are still friends. I dated Marcus for about a year before Russ came along. After breaking things off with Marcus, I met Russ and the rest is history. I love Russ and there is nothing really going on."

"Except the messages," says Sarah. "Laney told me that there have been some very interesting messages from him." I look over at Laney again, causing her to turn her face away.

"Yeah, there have been a few."

"Like what?" Sarah presses. "Come on, Tonya, don't be a fuddy-duddy. Give us the full details." She smiles as she looks at the other two women in our group. She apparently has their approval and support as she waits for my response.

"Marcus is lonely," I begin as I pick up my phone and find his messages. "Just keep that in mind." I hand it over to the three of them and wait as they scroll through our conversation. My face turns a hot, deep red as I bite my lower lip. The looks on their faces tell me that they are certainly interested in what they are reading.

"Damn, girl," Treena says before looking up at me. "He wants to do some shit with you, huh?"

"Yeah, I guess so," I reply.

"And so do you," Sarah observes. "You are a naughty little thing, Tonya."

"I don't know what I was thinking when I sent those messages to him. I guess since I have been married to Russ I have had to accept that things would be a little less fun."

"You are having sex with the dear hubby, right?" Laney asks.

I nod my head. "Of course we have sex, but it's just not as good as what I had with Marcus. He allowed me to be like a woman on fire. He encouraged me to try new things, and I miss that."

"So, Russ is boring?" Sarah clarifies.

"Not really *boring*. It's just that he's not as into some things as I am. I've tried to get him to be a little more adventurous, but nothing has worked so far."

"Well, whatever is or is not going on with you and Russ, this guy Marcus is really all about getting his groove on with you," Laney says with a giggle. "I wouldn't mind having a man like that plow my field."

"*Laney!*" The women laugh as I shake my head. "That's crass, sweetie."

"Yeah, well maybe I like crass," the youngest of us retorts. "You should give us his phone number and let us have a little fun with him too."

"Hey, that's an idea," Sarah says with a laugh. "Maybe Laney is onto something here."

"No, absolutely not," I reply. "Marcus would not appreciate having women he doesn't know texting him. Besides, you ladies are a little too tipsy to know what you are doing at the moment. I'm not giving you his phone number."

"Here it is." Treena sends a message from my cell phone to herself before passing my phone back to me.

"Don't do that," I plead with her as I watch her text the other two women the information.

Treena looks up at me. "You really shouldn't be playing around with this guy, Tonya. He broke your heart."

"And you shouldn't be texting him," I say as I watch her send a message to my ex-boyfriend. "Shit, Treena."

"Oh, I sent a good one," Laney says with a huge smile on her face. "I told him I could ride his face."

"Shit," Sarah laughs. "I wonder what I could say." She looks around and smiles before lifting her crop top and bra.

"What the fuck are you doing?!" I say as I shake my head. "Someone will see you."

"I hope so," she replies while taking a quick selfie of her breast. Sarah then lowers her top and sends the picture to Marcus.

"Fuck!" I put my hands into my face as the other women do things equally cringeworthy. Why did Laney tell Sarah about Marcus? I thought she could keep this secret, though I should have known better.

"I got a message back," Laney says excitedly. "He wants to know who I am." She begins to type in a response.

"Don't make it worse," I beg her. "Just drop it."

"I told him that I am your friend," Laney says with a smile. "We're just having fun with this, right?"

"Uh-oh, he wants to know who I am," Sarah laughs. "I wonder if he liked the boob pic?"

"You are going to make this really bad for me if you keep this up," I tell them as I become a little angry. "You're messing around with something that you shouldn't be."

"It's cool," Sarah replies. "I told him that we are just having a little fun with him." Looking at Treena, she asks, "What did you say?"

She looks up at us. "I told him that he should be careful with what he is doing here. I told him that Tonya is a married woman."

"Dammit, Treena," I seethe. "You girls are pissing me off."

"Alright, we'll stop," Sarah promises.

"Shit." My phone buzzes and I pick it up. The message is from Marcus. "I'm ruined." As I begin to read the message, the others lean in close to me.

"Are there friends of yours messaging me right now?" Marcus asks in the message.

I reply, "Yeah, it's them. They are a little too happy after having some wine tonight. I'm so sorry about that."

"Even the picture of the breast?" he asks. My heart beats hard as I look over at Sarah.

"Hey, it's just a boob. I didn't take a picture of my pussy and send it, did I?" Although she jokes a little about this, I have known her to send all sorts of pics to various men, including those of her muff.

"Yeah, Sarah sent that," I finally answer him. "She's sorry if you are offended."

"Offended?" Marcus sends a laughing emoji. "She has two of them, right?" he jokes.

"Oh, yeah, how rude of me," Sarah says after reading the message. She quickly lifts her top again and takes another selfie, this time of the other breast, and sends it to Marcus.

"A guy over there saw you do that just now," Treena informs our friend. We look over and see the man smile before he turns away, his face red. "Yep, you just made his night."

"I'm a giving woman," Sarah laughs. "Oh, a reply." She reads it to us. "Nice breasts. I like breasts."

"Oh, fuck," I say as I put my hand over my face. "This has gotten too embarrassing."

"Yeah, we need to knock it off," Treena says as she puts her phone down. "This guy was a real jerk to her back in the day and I don't want to see him mess with her like that again."

"I can take care of myself," I tell her before my phone buzzes in my hand again. Opening up the message from Marcus, I am shocked at what I see.

"Shit, is that his?" Laney says as she crowds in to see the picture he has sent.

"I can't believe he sent that," I say as my face turns even redder.

"A cock pic," Sarah laughs. "That is a nice one, girl. You need to ride the shit out of that one."

"She has," Treena interjects. "He knows better than that. You're married now, Tonya."

"I know," I say with some frustration while the other women enjoy the picture a moment longer.

"I would let him park that bus in my garage anytime," Laney quips, which causes the rest of us to gasp and then laugh.

"That's just...wow." Treena shakes her head as she laughs. "Laney, you are a dirty little thing."

"I'm a horny little thing." She smiles at me before asking, "Are you going to fuck him, Tonya? I mean, at least let him give you a little something just for kicks."

"Just for kicks," Sarah parrots as she runs her fingers through her hair. "We could tag team him, you know. Just me and you, Tonya."

"And me," Laney chimes in.

"This is a nightmare," I say as I pull my phone to me and lock it. "You ladies have made this a lot more difficult now. I don't know what to say to him or how to keep things where they have been after you have done all this." My heart beats fast as I think of Marcus and his large penis. There was a time when he could slide into me with his manhood and touch my cervix easily. He could bring me to an orgasm with just his long manhood within a matter of a couple of minutes. I have yet to experience anything like that with Russ, and so I miss it. I *really* miss it.

"You need to be careful here, girl. Things could get really confusing for you two if you aren't careful. If Russ finds out..."

"He's not going to find out," I interrupt Treena. "I lock my phone. He has no access to my text messages."

"It would only take one slip," Treena remarks. "I don't want to see you hurt by that man again."

Sarah puts a hand on my shoulder. "She's right, you know? Just be sure to use protection so you don't end up with a bun in the oven. That would be really hard to explain away with your hubby."

"Yeah, great advice," I answer dryly. "I'll have to keep from getting knocked up. The thing is, I don't plan to have sex with Marcus. That's it. Enough said." I reach for my wine and finish off the glass. My mind now swimming with the image of his dick, I begin to wonder what it would be like to be with him again. Marcus was a great lover and the sort of man who could take me to great heights sexually. I fear that Russ could find out, though. I would never want that. I love my husband and always will, regardless of the way I feel about our sex together.

Chapter Four: A Bit of Snooping

I get home first and my wife is still out with her friends. Though a little tired from my time at the bar with the guys, I decide that I will wait up for her after my shower. Honestly, I am not all that certain that I could go to sleep before she gets home anyway. Settling into our bed, I rest a while as I look on my phone at social media. I do not have to wait very long as I look up to see Tonya walk into the room.

"Late night?" I say with a smile on my face. Tonya has obviously had a bit too much wine with her meal, her face flushed.

"We stayed out way too late," she replies as she walks over to the bed and sits down on the edge. Looking at me, my wife asks, "Did they show up this time?"

I shrug my shoulders. "Just Adrian and Theo. Mike was a no-show again." I laugh. "His wife has a tight rein on him."

"Maybe I should have one on you too." Tonya giggles before bending down and kissing me. As she sits back up, she tells me, "I'll take a quick shower and be back out for bed in a few."

I watch her stand up before I get an idea. "Why don't you take a nice bath instead? You look like you could use a little relaxation, my love," I say as I reach out and take her hand. "Just soak in the water with one of those bath nukes."

"Bath *nukes?*" Tonya laughs. "They are called bath *bombs,* sweetheart. A bath would be really nice about now."

"I'll be right here," I tell her. "I had a shower earlier, so I'm good. Go enjoy yourself." I pat my wife on the ass and smile at her. She nods her head and walks toward the bathroom. It takes only a minute or so for the bath water to start and I realize that I have gone from ten minutes to an hour or more of time to do what I want to do. Getting out of the bed, I go to the dresser where she has put down her phone and car keys. Picking up the phone, I unlock it and begin to look at her text messages.

"Oh, shit, there are more," I say as I look at her conversation with the other man. This time, there is a picture of someone's penis as well. "You fucker," I say of the man as I look at the large sausage on display. Seeing that Marcus has asked about some text messages from her friends, I go to Tonya's conversations with the ladies on her cell phone. Several text messages have flurried in over the last several minutes.

"You should totally bang that guy," Sarah texted to my wife. "He's got a nice package and he could reach places inside you that Russ can't." I feel my face turn red as a woman I barely know questions my sexual prowess and my cock size. "You can keep it quiet, girl. Do him!" A devilish emoji is to the side of the message as I scroll on to another text in the group of women.

"Marcus is bad for you, Tonya. Don't do it. Get away from him. You do remember how he dumped you last time, right?" Treena said to her. I know Treena, and though I do not consider her a close friend of mine, her reputation with me has just gone up a notch.

"Fuck." My heart skips a beat as I shake my head. "Her old boyfriend." Now it all makes perfect sense to me. The man my wife has been sexting with is the last lover she had before me. Swallowing hard, I realize how bad this could be for me and my marriage to Tonya. Marcus is an old flame that I had hoped she had moved on from. Apparently she has not.

"Give him head," Laney says in her message to my wife. "What can it hurt? Russ will never know and you will have a good time. Oh, and he can eat you out too!" I shake my head as I scroll through and see several other messages from her friends that say pretty much the same things. They know about Tonya's text messages to a man who is not her husband and two of them think she should have sex with him behind my back. My wife's responses do not seem to dismiss the thought of doing that.

"Marcus was nice," she replied to them in a message. "But I'm married. I love Russ, not Marcus. Nothing is going to happen." Two emotions fill me at this moment. One is a sort of pride and love that I have for Tonya. The other is what I can only describe as disappointment.

"Why?" I ask myself as I look into the mirror on the wall above the dresser. "Are you some kind of sexually warped guy?" My mind has been wondering what it would be like for my wife to fuck Marcus. Sure, that would be crazy on any level, but something about her doing that makes me hard. Even now my cock is stiff and throbbing over the thought of it. "You dirty man," I say to myself as I put down my wife's phone. Turning toward the bed, I walk over and sit down. I then reach for my cell phone and begin to research information about men like me. It does not take long for me to find what I am looking for.

"This is insane," I say as I read an article about men who have wanted their wives to have sex with other men, including their ex-boyfriends or ex-spouses. Though the idea of it sounds foreign to me, I cannot help but enjoy the thought of Tonya's naked body in the embrace of another man. Just as she said to Marcus in one of her earlier messages, she could put her feet on his shoulder as he pushes into her small pussy.

"Fuck." I pre-come a little inside my shorts before I hear some movement in the bathtub.

"Russ," I hear my wife call out. I get up from the bed and walk into the bathroom.

"Hey, honey," I say as I muster a smile for her.

"Could you wash my back for me?" Tonya smiles at me as she holds up a bar of soap and washcloth. Nodding my head, I go to the bathtub and kneel beside it. As I begin to wash her back, my wife starts to talk to me about her friends.

"You know, the girls can sometimes be so crude when they get a little too much to drink."

"A little too much? Weren't you all at a restaurant?"

"Yeah, but they don't stop the wine from flowing there," Tonya replies. "Sarah was the worst of them tonight." I nod my head as if I understand. Actually, I do, as she was the one making the crudest of the suggestions to Tonya in her text messages.

"They are your *best* friends, though, right?"

"Of course they are," she answers. "I just wish that they would sometimes keep their comments to themselves."

I chuckle. "Well, as bad as your friends can be, I'm sure mine can be even worse. Men are notorious for the way they talk sometimes. That's especially true after they have been drinking." I run the washcloth over Tonya's back as I think about how sexy she is. Her skin is smooth and soft. I love to help her bathe.

"They were talking about some guy and his package," she confides in me. "It was not a great thing to do at a restaurant." Tonya pauses before adding, "Sarah actually took a picture of her boobs and sent it to the guy."

I stop washing her back. "What?"

"She took pics of her boobs, Russ. I would have never thought that she would do that, but she did. Sarah sent some guy she didn't know a picture of her breasts."

"Geez," I laugh. "That never happens to me."

Tonya laughs along with me. "Well, I'm sure Sarah would be happy to do that for you. At least, she might be willing to do that after she has had a few too many glasses of wine." My wife smiles as she shakes her head. "They were so bad tonight. I hope you are okay with me seeing them."

"What? Why wouldn't I be?" I sit down on the floor beside the bathtub and watch as Tonya lays back in the soapy water.

"I don't know. You trust me so much, don't you?" Her beautiful face turns toward me and her eyes study my expression. "Sometimes I forget just how great a guy you are, Russ. I am really lucky to have you." She reaches toward me and puts a hand behind my neck. My wife gives me a passionate kiss as she runs her wet fingers through my hair. After she finishes, she lets me go and I sit back.

"You're a wonderful wife," I tell her as Marcus is still on my mind. "I couldn't have done any better than you. I love you, Tonya."

"I love you too." We smile at each other for a moment before she tells me, "I'll be out in a little. Could you have the lights ready for us?"

"Um, sure." I smile widely as I get up from the floor. Whenever she asks me to have the lights ready, Tonya means that she wants me to adjust the ambience of the room. We are going to have sex tonight and my manhood is more than ready to feel her tight pussy around it. Getting up from the floor, I leave the bathroom and look over at the dresser where her phone is lying. I have discovered a lot over the last couple of days from that little device.

"I wonder if you would really fuck him?" I say quietly as I look over at the bathroom door. "Would you put your feet on his shoulders so that he could get deep inside you?" Though I ask this, I know that Tonya cannot hear me. It would not be in my best interest for her to know that I know everything at this point. No, I want to have a little fun with my wife tonight. The last thing I want to do is cause any drama between us by admitting that I have been getting into her cell phone and reading her text messages. Tonight will be a nice night between just the two of us.

I hear the bathtub draining as I take off my clothes and dim the lights in the bedroom. After lying back on the bed, I gently stroke my cock and wait for Tonya to come to me. Knowing that I will have Marcus and his large equipment in my mind while I penetrate my wife, I plan to use that to my advantage. Maybe after tonight she will see a good fucking with me as something that compares well with whatever she had with her ex-boyfriend a few years ago. Then again, I may suck at having sex. Whatever happens, I intend to come inside Tonya. I am going to come really hard.

Chapter Five: Found Out

I decide to cook breakfast for Tonya as she sleeps in the bedroom. It is after ten in the morning and my head aches a little from a lack of sleep. The thought of the text messages and the way my wife has kept everything from me is enough to keep my thoughts fixed on nothing else. Why do I feel so turned on by the thought of her with her old boyfriend? Most guys would undoubtedly find that sort of thing disgusting if it happened with their wives or girlfriends. Though I am bothered a little by it, I feel as if I would welcome seeing Tonya have sex with Marcus.

"You're up early," my sleepy spouse says as she walks into the kitchen. "Oh, wow. You made pancakes?" A smile forms on her face as she has a seat on a stool beside the kitchen island.

"I had trouble sleeping," I say honestly. "So, I figured you could use a little something special today." I slide a plate with three pancakes over to her and then get the syrup. After I place it in front of her plate, I sit down and smile at her.

Tonya takes a quick bite of her pancakes after putting a bit of syrup on them. "This is really good," she says with a smile while chewing her food. "You're so sweet for doing this, Russ." My wife seems genuinely appreciative of the effort I have put forth to give her a nice breakfast.

"I'm glad you like them," I say as I look at the pancakes on her plate. "It's a recipe I found online. There's some sour cream in the mix to make them fluffier."

My wife looks up at me. "I love it. It looks like you will be our chef for breakfast from now on." We both laugh for a moment before Tonya realizes there is something going on in my mind. "What is it, Russ?"

Sighing, I straighten up on my stool before asking her, "You know that I love you, right?" Looking nervously at my wife, I wait for her reply.

"We said that to each other last night, Russ. I love you very much. You are my wonderful man." She smiles at me, which makes what I am about to say a little more difficult.

"I know, Tonya. I've known for a few days." There is a quietness in the kitchen as my wife's eyes focus on me.

"You know what?" She seems confused at what I mean as she puts down her fork.

"About *him*," I say as my heart skips a few beats. "You have tried to keep me in the dark about him, but I know."

"Russ, I don't know what you are talking about."

"Marcus," I blurt out before taking a deep breath. I watch as Tonya's face turns white as she looks away. "I've seen the messages between the two of you."

My wife shakes her head. "You don't know what you're talking about, sweetheart. There is no one in my life right now by that name."

"Honey," I say while shaking my head. "I just told you that I have seen the text messages. I know you have been talking to your ex-boyfriend. Some of the messages were really sexual." Tonya appears to try to catch her breath as she realizes that I know all about Marcus. I can see that her mind is working on a response, but what can she say that is not the truth?

"Russ, I..." Her voice trails off as she rethinks what she is about to say. I have her in a corner and there really is no other way to approach this than to be completely honest with me. "We haven't been together."

Shaking my head, I ask, "What is that supposed to mean? Do you mean that so far you haven't had sex with your old boyfriend since sexting with him?" Though I am aroused by the idea that she would like to fuck Marcus, I am also a little upset that the sexting has gone on behind my back.

"Wait," Tonya says as she narrows her eyes and looks at me. "How did you see the text messages?"

"Your phone," I say without hesitation. "I found them there."

"My *phone?*" My wife purses her lips. "How the hell did you get into my cell phone, Russ? That's *my* phone, not yours!"

"Your password is our wedding date," I say as I shake my head. "Don't try to make this about me, honey. The fact of the matter is you are in some kind of sexual relationship with your ex-boyfriend behind my back."

"We are not having sex!" Tonya replies loudly as she pushes her plate of pancakes away. "How dare you? How dare you look through my phone?!" She looks around the kitchen as if she is planning her next move. Thankfully, the knives are put away in a drawer behind me.

"You're sexting with him. You might as well screw the guy, Tonya," I retort. "And those fucking friends of yours want you to do it, right? Laney and that other one…Sarah. They want you to have sex with him behind my back like it's no big deal. Only Treena seems to have any sense about what is right and wrong."

"But, you went through my *phone!* That's my personal property, dammit!" My wife is livid as she clenches her fists. "I can't believe you are so sneaky."

"*Sneaky?* Seriously, my love? Which of us happens to be sneakier? The one who happens to figure out a PIN number that's a wedding date or the one who is sending sexually explicit messages to a man who is not married to her?!" I raise my voice as I think of the messages between all of the individuals involved. I am angry, but I am also horny as I think about Tonya with the other man.

"Russ." My wife stops herself for a moment as she looks down at her hands. Calming down a little, she asks, "What are you going to do? Are you going to leave me?"

"I never said that," I reply. "Not one time have I thought about leaving you, Tonya. I just don't understand what is going on here. Who brought Marcus back into your life? Was it you or one of the girls?"

"I don't know that there is a clear answer to that," she begins while shaking her head. "I just happened to think of him a while back and I sent him a message to see how things were going. One thing led to another and here we are." Tonya turns her blues eyes to look into mine. Tears are filling them and I begin to feel terrible for the way I have spoken to her. Perhaps I could have gone a different route with this? Surely we could have gone to see a marriage counselor and then I could have brought what I knew to that conversation.

"So, you aren't trying to get back with him?" I ask.

"No, dammit." My wife is still angry with me, as well she should be. We have both violated each other's trust in some way and it will take time for the two of us to be back to any sense of mutual trust in our relationship.

"Did you send him any nudes?"

"What?"

"Nudes. He sent you a dick pic, Tonya. Did you send him something to even things out?"

"Fuck, Russ, you are so full of yourself." She gets up from her stool, her face once again drawn into an angry form. "You went into my phone and found things that are not yours to find, then you ask me if I am showing myself off to another man."

"It's a legitimate question," I reply.

"He's my *ex-boyfriend*. He's seen everything that I have already. What would it matter if I sent him a naked picture?" Tonya looks angrily at me and says before I can answer, "You know what? *FUCK IT!* I don't have to explain anything to you, Russ. I'm a big girl and I will do whatever I want. I've told you there hasn't been any sex with Marcus, so you can either believe me or don't believe me. I don't have to sit here for this." My wife turns and walks toward our bedroom. I get up from my stool and follow her there as I hear her curse at me.

"I'm not trying to pick at you, honey, but you have to admit that when a husband finds that sort of thing it is bound to make him a little nervous. All I am asking is that you shut things down with him. There's no reason for you to be talking to your old boyfriend anyway." This sounds like a very sane request to me, but Tonya does not appear to be equally inclined.

She stops and turns to look at me just inside our bedroom. "If you don't like what I am doing, you can leave."

"*Leave?*" I shake my head. "I have already told you that I'm not looking for that sort of thing, Tonya. There's no reason for you to be like this." She does not respond as she finds some clothes and puts them on. In minutes, my wife has left the house and I am confused as to how I could have handled that better.

"What the fuck just happened?" I ask the empty air of our living room. Turning, I pick up my cell phone and look up Marcus Hannigan on social media. The old boyfriend has several posts that I have already been looking at. There has to be some clue as to what his intentions are with her since he has taken it upon himself to talk to her behind my back. As I look at one of the social media sites where he has a presence, I realize that Marcus is married and has a baby girl.

"No way," I say with a chuckle. "You are going after your old girlfriend even though you have a baby with another woman? What is wrong with you?" My emotions simmer for a moment as I think about this revelation. "Does Tonya know?" I ask as I look at the pictures of the baby on Marcus's page. "You sly dog." Scrolling through the site, I finally find a picture of his young wife as well. An attractive woman, there is no way that someone like Marcus would find her boring. He must have a real thing for Tonya if he is talking to her now.

I grit my teeth as I send a text message to Tonya. "Where are you going?"

For a few moments it seems that she might not answer. However, I soon get a response. "Going to see a friend. Maybe she will understand." That is all I hear from my wife as I sit down on the sofa.

"Dammit, I could have handled that so much better," I chastise myself. "We didn't have to end our conversation like that. There's so much more that could have been said if I had just thought it out better. I hope she doesn't leave me." My stomach feels tight as I consider for a moment what life would be like without Tonya. She is everything to me and I do not want to lose her to another man who already has his own wife. Without Tonya I would be rudderless; a ship lost at sea. As horny as I am to see her have sex with him, I want more than anything else that I will not lose her to Marcus Hannigan or any other man.

Chapter Six: Worried Sick

My heart has been pounding ever since I left the house this morning. What can I do? What do I say to Russ to let him know that Marcus is not a man that I love. I just *want* him. "Fuck me," I say quietly as I drive around the city. For two hours I have roamed the streets in my car, stopping for a few minutes at a city park before getting back inside and driving aimlessly along yet more streets. "This sucks so bad, Tonya. You've really screwed up with this. What the hell were you thinking? You should have never messaged Marcus in the first place."

I pull into the driveway of a small, light blue house on the other side of town and get out of my car. It is almost noon and I can only hope that my friend is at home. As I walk up to the front door of the house, it suddenly opens and out steps Treena.

"Hey, what are you doing here?" she asks as she motions for me to come inside. I step into her living room as she closes the door behind me.

"He knows," I say as tears begin to build in my eyes. "Russ knows everything. I don't know what to do." Treena steps quickly toward me and takes me into her arms. She knows what I mean as she puts a hand on the back of my head and allows me to rest my chin on her shoulder.

"I was worried this would happen," she says quietly while comforting me. "How did he find out?" Treena releases me from her embrace and I step back as I clutch my hands together.

"My cell phone. Russ broke into my phone and found the text messages. He knows everything." I suck in a couple of quick breaths as I try to calm myself. "I told him that it didn't mean anything, but he doesn't really believe me. He's going to leave me, Treena. I know he is."

My friend shakes her head. "I don't believe that for one second, sweetie," she replies. "Russ loves you very much. It's going to take some time to smooth things out, but he'll come around eventually. You haven't actually *done* anything with Marcus, right?"

I shake my head. "That doesn't matter to Russ. He said that I might as well have. He knows my history with Marcus and now he knows that I miss having sex with him. Russ even saw the penis picture he sent to me."

"Oh, that's not good," Treena says with a sigh. "Here, let's have a seat," she says to me while guiding me toward a couch nearby. We sit down beside each other and she puts an arm around me. "Was he very angry?"

I shrug. "I think he was. I don't know. There was a flurry of things said back and forth between us and I think that maybe I got a little more angry than he did." I think about how I yelled at my husband for getting into my phone and reading my text messages with Marcus and my friends. "Maybe I went too far with how I responded? I don't know, Treena. I was so pissed off that he went through my phone."

"And you made it more about that, right?" She looks at me with understanding eyes as she pats my knee with her hand. "Russ should have never read your text messages, but to be honest, if you don't have trust between the two of you then you don't have a marriage, Tonya. Just ask my ex-husband about that." Treena was married to a man for more than five years before asking him to leave. She loved him but she had become tired of his constant lying about little things he would sometimes do. The lies were far worse to her than anything he had actually done, but they were enough to convince my friend that her marriage was over.

"I fucked up, Treena. I fucked up when I messaged Marcus a few weeks ago and I fucked up again when I yelled at Russ for getting into my cell phone. Maybe I overreacted a little."

Treena sighs as she looks into my eyes. "Look, there are lots of things in a marriage that can come between two people and cause them problems, Tonya. This is one of many. You just have to figure out what you need to do to make things better with Russ." Pausing for a moment to gauge my expression, she asks, "Should you message Marcus and tell him that this is over?"

Something inside me cringes as I think about breaking off my conversations with my old boyfriend. Why should I? It is not as if we are having sex together. Our text messages are hot and a lot of fun, but they are not the sort of thing that I think I should have to give up just because Russ has snuck into my phone and found them. What right does he have to tell me who I can talk to? Or what I can say to them? I talk to Treena, Sarah, and Laney all the time. Do I have to cut them off as well?

"I don't want to," I confess to Treena. "He's a nice guy and we're not doing anything wrong by just talking through text messages."

"Sweetie, I don't think your hubby is thinking of this in the same way that you are. This could hurt your marriage if you keep it up. You will need to make a choice." Treena is the most pragmatic of my friends. Her level head and gentle way with me has helped me to make some very important decisions before. However, I can't see this decision as being one that I want to make.

"What if I tell Russ that I have broken off contact with him. I could keep texting Marcus and just keep it quiet."

"Russ will find out again, Tonya."

"Not if he can't get into my cell phone. I've already changed the password, Treena. He will never be able to figure it out now." Though I know better, I try to make an argument with my friend that sounds completely sane and rational. Unfortunately, I can see by the look on her face that she does not feel the same about my plan.

"Don't do it, Tonya," Treena tells me while shaking her head. "Keeping this from Russ in the first place has already gotten you into a little trouble with him. Doing it again, if you get caught..."

"I won't," I insist. "I can do this. I know I can."

"And you thought that you could do that in the first place, too. Tonya, you are a grown woman and you will have to make this decision on your own. I can't make it for you. All I can do is give you some advice based on my own experiences with Dave. Lies were all I had to look forward to with that man, and it brought our marriage down. Doing that to Russ isn't fair and you know it. Just think everything through really well before you decide to do that, okay? Promise me that much."

"I promise," I reply as I wipe my eyes and smile at Treena.

"And you aren't falling in love with Marcus again, are you?"

"Hell no," I reply while shaking my head. "I was never really in love with him in the first place. Everything was about one thing."

"*Sex,*" Treena chuckles. I nod my head. "Well, I guess that's something to base a relationship on. Just don't do that to Russ now that you are married to him. If you are going to keep Marcus around just for dirty talk, fine, but don't screw him behind your husband's back. That would not be right at all."

"I know. I don't want to have sex with Marcus anyway. I love Russ and I know that would bring a whole new problem to our marriage that we would probably not be able to fix. It was fun with the ex when we were together, but things have changed so much for both of us. I have changed."

"And Marcus has a kid with a wife," Treena unloads as if I did not already know that. "Seriously?" she says as she looks at my face. "You have known all along about the wife and kid, haven't you?"

"I found out when I looked him up. Remember, I'm the one who first messaged Marcus."

"And you still think this is okay? To carry on like this and for the two of you to both put your marriages on the line?"

"His wife is cool with him sexting with other women. To her, that is apparently the best way to keep Marcus from cheating on her."

"You spoke to his wife?" Treena says with surprise.

"No, of course not," I say with a smirk. "Marcus filled me in on her and how she is fine with the whole sexting thing. She just doesn't want any details. Though I think he would love to take things further, I'm not going to allow it. This has all just been for fun, not the rekindling of something that has been gone for three years now. We have both moved on with our lives."

Moved on," Treena huffs with a strained look on her face. "I don't think the two of you have moved on as much as you might think you have. Just be careful, Tonya. I love you like a sister and I don't want to see you or Russ hurt. As for Marcus, I really don't give a shit about him." We both laugh for a moment before I get up from the couch. Treena does the same and follows me to the door.

"Thank you for listening to me rant," I tell her. "You really are a great friend, Treena. You always give me great advice."

"And you rarely take it," she observes with a smile. "Be good, girl. I'll see you later." We hug once more before I turn around and walk back to my car. Pulling my phone out of my pants pocket, I unlock it and send Marcus a quick message.

"Are you available for a quick talk?" Getting into my car, I start the engine and just sit in the air conditioning for a minute or so. Marcus answers me back and I read the text message.

"I'm here."

Sighing, I type in my message to him. "Russ knows about us. He got into my phone and found our messages to each other." My hand shakes as I send the text message to my ex-boyfriend.

"Damn," he replies simply.

"We need to keep our texts quiet, okay? Don't text my friends at all. They can't know that we are still talking, Marcus." Again, my hand shakes as I send this message. Though I am not hooking up with him physically, I want to continue my dirty little chats with my ex. They help me get through the day sometimes when I feel that Russ has not spent enough time with me.

"I can do that," he promises. "Are you in trouble with your husband?"

"A little," I admit. "I am going to tell him there will be no more messages between us. Hopefully we can keep this as our little secret."

"My lips are sealed," he replies quickly. "Don't worry, babe, it will be alright." A smiling emoji follows the text message.

Smiling to myself, I answer, "I'll text you later, okay?" I send my own emoji with a huge smile on its face before I put the cell phone down and back out of Treena's driveway. Turning toward home, I think about my conversation with my friend and how badly I want to keep having my dirty little text message conversations with Marcus. Treena is not as convinced as I am about keeping this going, but she would surely feel differently if she were the one texting an old boyfriend of hers. Then again, I have known her to be able to cut off her feelings for old flings fairly quickly. Maybe she would never allow herself to be in my situation at all. Still, I want what I want and I think I can do this without worrying about Russ finding out again. At least, I intend to try.

Chapter Seven: A Fantasy in Mind

Tonya comes into our bedroom after getting back from her friend's house. I have wondered all day which friend's house in particular she went to, but I avoid asking as I look at her and try to figure out what state of emotion she is in at the moment.

"Hey," I say quietly as Tonya puts her things down on the dresser nearby.

She looks at me briefly and replies, "Hey." She then goes into the bathroom and begins to take off her clothes. I follow and try to start a conversation with my wife.

"Are you alright? I mean, after we talked this morning, I wasn't sure that you were coming back." A lump forms in my throat as I imagine how easily Tonya could have left me if she had wanted to do so.

"I'm fine," she replies before telling me, "I went to see Treena. She had some good advice." Tonya begins to take off her clothes after starting the shower.

"Oh, really?" I get hard as I watch my wife's bra hit the floor nearby. Her small, firm breasts are beautiful and begging for me to touch them. However, I keep my distance as I continue to talk to her.

"Yeah. She told me to break it off with him. So, I'm going to do it. Will this make things better between us, Russ?" Tonya's blue eyes stare at me for a moment as she stands topless in front of me.

Nodding my head, I answer, "I guess so." I am relieved on the one hand that my wife is willing to break off her virtual relationship with her old boyfriend, but on the other hand I wish she would just fuck him. I want her to fuck him while I watch her do it. What is wrong with me? Why would I want this?

"Good. I'm sorry I was so upset with you this morning, Russ. I didn't mean for things to go like that. Marcus and I had a pretty intense thing at one time, you know? Maybe I shouldn't have texted him, but I did, and I am sorry for that. I'll stop talking to him immediately." She manages a short smile before taking off her pants and thong panties. My cock begins to ooze pre-come as I see her nude body in front of me. I want so badly to pull her away from the shower and fuck her over the sink.

"It's alright. I love you."

"I love you too." Tonya turns and gets into the shower and closes the door behind her. I stand and watch her through the clear plexiglass for a couple of minutes. She is a beautiful woman, a spinner at just five-four and one hundred twenty pounds. My wife, the sexual dynamo that she is, would undoubtedly prefer to have sex with Marcus if she had the opportunity. It would be fun to watch her do that, but I do not want to bring that up with her. If I were to ask her to actually bring him over for a quick romp, what would that say about me? Would it mean that I am nothing but a hypocrite after what happened between us this morning? I ache to say something to her, but I cannot. So, I make my way back into the bedroom and sit down in a chair.

Looking at Tonya's cell phone on the dresser nearby, I know better than to try to open it and look at her messages. She has most likely changed her phone's password which means that any effort would likely be futile. Though she tells me that she will stop her communications with her ex-boyfriend, I doubt my wife's sincerity. No, she will likely keep talking to him behind my back. Now that she can hide it from me, Tonya has no reason to worry that I will find out about any new text messages between the two of them.

Tonya comes out of the bathroom a few minutes later and walks into the bedroom. She is still nude and glistening as she dries herself with a large bath towel. "Pull it out, sweetheart," she says to me.

"What?" I laugh.

"Your dick, Russ. Pull your shorts down so that I can see it." I begin to harden again as I do as my wife asks. My throbbing manhood springs out of the thin fabric of my shorts and Tonya walks up to me before kneeling down. Her hands carefully wrap around it and she begins to pump it for me.

"Shit, honey," I moan as I watch her playing with my shaft. "Is this how we are going to make up?"

Tonya giggles. "I could see how hard you were in the bathroom, dummy. You need a quick release." My wife continues to rub my cock with her soft hands. I pre-come a little and she takes the slippery mess to rub it around the end of my shaft. Gripping the arms of the chair, I enjoy the feeling of her small, soft hands on my johnson.

"Spit on it," I say with a groan. My wife smiles before putting a little saliva on the head of my cock and then running her hands over it. The feeling of her hands and the lubricant from her mouth on my pole causes me to move around in the chair. Tonya moves her hands a little faster up and down my full length as she smiles at me.

"Is that good?" she asks with a wicked smile on her face.

"Fuck, yeah," I say before gritting my teeth. My toes begin to point as the intensity of her teasing mounts. "Shit, you're going to make me come, Tonya."

She laughs. "That's the point, right? To get my hubby to come for me?" My wife smiles as she watches my manhood flex inside her hands. She can tell when I am getting close to losing my load.

"Oh, honey," I growl as I feel my jism working its way from my balls to the tip of my peter. "Honey, I'm going to..." I close my eyes as I feel the orgasm overtake me suddenly. *AHHHH!!!* The first spurt launches and lands on my wife's arm, causing her to flinch a little as the second spurt comes out. *"Fuck...ohhhhh...uhhhh...ohhhh..."* I come hard as she allows my spunk to spill out all over her hands and arms. *"Tonya...FUCK!!!"* My mind races with images of the large cock in my wife's text messages being shoved into her tiny twat. I want her to fuck Marcus. I would beg her to do it if I thought she would not become upset that I had suddenly changed my mind about him. *"Uhhhh..."*

"What a mess," my wife laughs as she pulls her hands up my stalk to express the last bit of my man gravy out of me.

"Shit, honey," I say as I try to catch my breath. "Holy shit, that was so fucking intense."

Tonya smiles at me. "Yeah, you really had a nice one this time. I guess make up hand jobs are the best?" She laughs a little and I do as well before we both lose our smiles. Getting up from the end of the bed, my wife turns and walks into the bathroom. She has done a great job of cleaning me off with her hands, so all I have to do is pull up my shorts. After I do, I walk into the bathroom to talk to her.

"That was very nice, Tonya. Can I do something for you? I wouldn't mind having a taco for dinner, if you know what I mean."

She smiles at me as she dries her hands. "Thanks, sweetie, I appreciate the offer. I don't think that I'm really in the mood for that right now, though." Tonya reaches for a tee shirt nearby and drops it over her head. It is a bit large for her, which means it covers her upper torso very well. With this shirt she does not need a pair of panties to cover her bottom half.

"I hope it's not something I said or did," I reply. "I know that I should have never gotten into your text messages, Tonya. I only did it after I saw a notification come through with a guy's name I didn't recognize. That's really no excuse, but I want you to know why I did what I did. I wasn't just randomly snooping behind your back."

Tonya nods her understanding. "I should have never contacted him in the first place. You don't deserve having me do that to you, sweetheart." My wife seems sincere in what she says, but I still have a hard time believing that she will completely cut Marcus off. Though I want to tell her my fantasy about him fucking her, I decide that doing so might not be best. I do not want to make things any worse between us right now.

"Well, if you don't want to allow me to have a taco for dinner right now, maybe I should make you dinner? Would you like that?"

Tonya nods her head. "I think that would be great, Russ. I can help, too."

"No, I can do it. You just sit down in the living room and turn on the television. Find a show that we can watch together, alright? Maybe a movie?"

"Yeah, I can do that." She walks up to me and gives me a quick kiss before leaving the bedroom. My cock flexes a little as it becomes semi-hard inside my shorts. "Fuck him for me," I say under my breath after Tonya leaves our bedroom. "Just do it so that I can watch. Fuck Marcus." I want so badly to ask her to do this, but I could never do such a thing. Our marriage needs to heal from the loss of trust we have both suffered recently. Though I would love to show Tonya that I can be sexually adventurous by offering a tryst between her and her former lover, I know that I will have to tread lightly for now. We have a lot to do to get our marriage back on level ground and I will avoid doing anything that could endanger that.

Chapter Eight: Something Worth Doing

The shower was a welcome opportunity for me to think about what has happened today. A whirlwind of emotions have swept over me since talking to Russ this morning and with Treena's advice on my mind I feel as if I am caught in a tough spot. I want to keep Marcus on the side for a little sex talk and maybe even some picture trading, but there is something more that I have tried to ignore. There is something much deeper that I yearn for with my old boyfriend that could be the sort of thing that might really upset Russ if I mention it to him.

Giving Russ a hand job was my way to get his mind off Marcus and what has been going on between us. Maybe it was also my way of trying to make things up with my husband. Even so, sex with my old boyfriend was fantastic when I was with him and I cannot forget it. He could bring me to an orgasm with just his cock inside my pussy. Even Russ has a hard time doing that, causing me to have to help out by playing with my clit while he thrusts in and out of me. It is not my husband's fault, though. He has a slightly smaller dick than my former boyfriend, though not by much. Maybe part of the reason I had such an easier time with my ex is the way Marcus would simply take me as if I was his property. The dirty, passion-soaked fuckery that went on between us was simply beyond anything else I have experienced before I met him or since. Had I met Russ and never known Marcus, I would think that my husband was the most magnificent lover in the world. Unfortunately, he has had a lot to live up to in our marriage.

After putting on my bathrobe, I make my way to the living room. Russ has decided to go in there and have a seat on the sofa while the television is on with the news. Though he does not make watching the news a habit, my husband likes to use the television to take his mind off other things when he is bothered by something. I know what that something is, which is why I sit down beside him to talk to him.

"Russ," I say as I put a hand on his knee. "Is everything alright between us?"

He turns and smiles at me, his dark brown eyes peering into mine. "Everything is fine, honey. I just hope you can say the same thing."

Swallowing first, I reply, "You know that you are everything to me, right? There is no other man who will ever have my heart, Russ. Only you have captured it."

He nods his head. "I know, Tonya. I have your heart, but I think someone else still captures your imagination, right?" It is a question that appears to be free of harsh judgment as my husband simply tries to get a better understanding of my mind on Marcus.

"We don't have to talk about this right now if you don't want to," I tell him. "I know that his name is probably the last name that you want to hear right now."

"Marcus," Russ replies as he looks down at my hand on his knee. Moving his hand to mine, he says, "I know you had a great thing with him at one time, Tonya. We've talked about your past relationship with him before."

I sigh. "But you don't know enough of the story to understand what is happening right now." Straightening myself beside him, I continue, "Marcus came along when I thought that no one wanted me. I mean, *truly* wanted me. I had boyfriends before him and I went on dates, but every single time I became intimate with a man he would just treat me like a one night stand and then be gone."

"You wanted someone to love you."

Smiling, I reply, "No, that's not it at all. I wasn't looking for love. All I wanted was to have a man who wanted me so badly that he got hard at the thought of me. I wanted someone who could have passionate sex with me and make me think that I was the only woman in the world."

"And I've disappointed you in that department," Russ says with a sigh.

"No, you haven't," I say quickly to him as I bring a hand up to his cheek. "Sweetheart, you love me more than anyone ever has. There is no way to deny that. The problem is that the passion that I had with Marcus was..."

"Deeper," my husband interrupts. "He was a better lover."

"Different," I reply. "It was very different. You are a gentle lover who cares about me and what I need. Marcus isn't exactly a gentle lover and he gave me more of what I want. My needs were secondary during my time with him."

"I don't get that," he replies. "What you want isn't what you need? You know that I want you to have the best sex ever with me, right? What can I do to make it better?" Russ looks into my eyes and a part of me wants to be completely honest right now. I want to fuck Marcus. I would not care if Russ saw us with each other as long as I could feel my ex-boyfriend's manhood buried deep inside me, my cervix rocking with each thrust. Do I tell him as much? Do I admit to my husband that I want to have sex with another man and then hope that he will let me do it without leaving me? I cannot do it.

"Russ, it's a bit more complicated than that. I have never loved Marcus or any other lover that I've had. I have only ever loved you. Surely you know that."

He looks up at the television for a moment before turning his face back to me. "I know that you love me, Tonya. I think sex between us is pretty good, but I can see where maybe someone else did it in a way that you liked a little better. If I could give you the same experience, I would." Looking into my husband's eyes, I can see that there is more that he would like to say to me. Why is he holding back? What is it that Russ wants to say? I wish he would be honest with me, even if that honesty were to hurt my feelings. I can take it. After all, I have just unloaded a lot onto him that I never expected to.

"What do we do now?" I ask as I settle back on the sofa with him.

Russ sits quietly for a moment before replying, "I guess it depends on what you and I both want. I do want you to have the sort of sex that you want to have, Tonya. I don't want to deprive you of something like that.

If only you could help me to understand how to do things better for you, I would be a quick learner."

I smile at my husband. "I know you would. Maybe we should try to make things more special between us. More exciting."

He nods his head. "I would like that. Tonya, all I want is to give you whatever you want, including in bed. I don't want to be selfish and imagine that everything has to be about me, so if that's what I have been doing, just tell me. Tell me what Marcus did for you that I could do."

"Sweetie, I don't want to compare the two of you."

"Just tell me," he begs. "What did he do that I could try to do to make things better for you in bed? I want to learn, honey. I want to have sex with you so that we have more passion too."

Taking a breath, I begin to shake as I reply, "He would just take me, Russ. You and I don't do that sort of thing for sex. You never take me."

"What do you mean by that?" he asks with a slight scowl on his face.

"Marcus would..." I stop as I look into Russ's eyes. The hesitation I feel is due to the fact that my husband sometimes does not like to hear how someone does something better than he does. I worry that he will take this the wrong way when I say it. "He would come up to me and literally turn me around, pull my shorts down, and fuck me before I could say one way or the other if I was in the mood."

"What?" Russ shakes his head. "You would slap me if I did that to you. Tonya, you hate surprises." He is right. I have pulled away from my husband a few times in the past when he has tried to get a little freaky with me. I suppose it was a timing thing with us, but I cannot be certain.

"I don't know why I was different with him than I am with you when it comes to that," I reply. "I just know that when Marcus wanted me, I could never resist him. He would start thrusting inside me and making me so wet that I would drool down my legs." I freeze for a moment as I realize what I have said to my husband. He sits quietly, his eyes fixed on me as he tries to understand where this is coming from.

"Okay." Russ shakes his head. "And what else? What else makes him so alluring, my love." I cannot tell whether my husband is being sarcastic or if he seriously wants to know. Assuming the latter, I decide to tell him more.

"Things were never planned. We would go out and then make out. Heavy petting, a little finger penetration, and then sex. We even had sex in a park in the middle of the day one time. It was completely unplanned, Russ. Everything we did was unplanned."

"Unplanned," Russ replies. "So, the two of you liked to be a little disorganized when having sex."

"No, it wasn't like that. We planned things too. However, Marcus and I liked to be spontaneous, Russ. If we were horny and we wanted to have sex, we had sex. It never mattered where we were or what we were doing at the time. We had sex." My heart races as I tell my husband the nitty gritty details of my sex life with my former boyfriend. Everything rolling out of my mouth now is the truth and it feels liberating to finally share this with him.

He looks up at the television again for a moment. There is something on the news about an airstrike in Syria. The blurb is not much, but it seems to captivate his attention for a moment. At least, that is what it seems like. My husband gets lost in the news sometimes while thinking through something else. My guess is that he is not certain how he should reply to what I have just told him.

Russ turns his gaze back to me. "I'm a different sort of guy, Tonya. I don't think I could just bend you over a shelf in a grocery store and have sex with you. We would get into a lot of trouble if we got caught."

"And maybe that's what the whole thing with Marcus was," I reply. "We didn't care what could happen. We went with what we wanted, no matter the consequences."

He chuckles as he shakes his head. "I wish I could do something to make your sex life better, Tonya. Be honest with me, what would make it better for you?" His brown eyes look into mine once again and I almost tell him that I would like to have one more fling with Marcus. Almost. I am unable to do it though as I study the expression on his face. Russ wants to say something else, but he holds back. If only he would just say what he wants to say. Everything could be better if we were both honest with each other. Unless it would not be better. Who knows at this point?

"I love you, Russ. That's all that matters to me right now. We are husband and wife and I am proud of that fact. Sex with you is great, sweetheart. Never tell yourself otherwise. What I had with Marcus was fun, but I have matured and decided on a different life. Marcus and I never loved each other, which made things a little easier when it came to breaking up with him. You came along and swept me off my feet, Russ. You will always be my knight in shining armor." I lean over and give my husband a kiss on his cheek. He turns and kisses me for a moment and we simply enjoy each other's presence.

He pulls back and tells me, "I love you, Tonya. I would be happy to do anything for you. Anything. All you have to do is ask." Russ smiles and stands up from the sofa. "I think I'm going to have a shower and go to bed a bit early. Would you like to join me in bed?"

I smile back at him. "Sure. I'll go to bed." He helps me to my feet and we walk back to the bedroom after turning off the television. Russ is a kind, loving man who means more than anything else in the world to me. Marcus will simply have to go back to his own life and stop texting with me. After the conversation I have just had with my husband, there simply is no other way to do this.

Chapter Nine: A Sudden Opportunity

I try to use work this morning to take my mind off what Tonya said to me last night, but I find it difficult to completely forget. She had intense sex with Marcus when she was with him a few years ago, and apparently I am unable to match him in bed. I want to feel hurt right now about the whole thing, but that would be the very opposite of how I actually feel. Last night I wanted to tell my wife that she could have sex with Marcus. One last hoorah with the boyfriend before cutting it all off was what I was prepared to offer her, but I could not do it. What would she have thought of me if I had?

A phone call comes through to my desk phone and I pick it up. "Russ?" I hear Tonya say on the other end.

"Hey, honey," I reply with a smile on my face.

She pauses before asking me, "Would you like to meet me at a hotel near here?"

"A hotel?" My cock gets hard as I consider the offer. "Right now? It's ten in the morning, Tonya. We both have work."

"We can take a day off, can't we?" she asks. "It will be worth your while, sweetheart. I promise." I can hear the pleading in her voice. Is Tonya trying to be spontaneous with me? Is this her way of trying to reenact something with me that would have taken place with her ex-boyfriend a few years ago?

"Yeah, we can do that," I reply as I feel my heart beating hard inside my chest. "Which hotel?"

"Hotel DeLaun," Tonya tells me. "Room two-fourteen."

"Wait, you already have a room?" I say with surprise.

"It's already booked, sweetie. Get there as soon as you can. We don't have much time, okay?"

"I'll go now," I promise as I smile to myself and adjust my growing bulge inside my pants. "I'll see you there." Hanging up the phone, I look over at the other people in my office. It has been a very long time since I have taken a day off, so I feel confident that the boss will be fine with it. Without pausing, I make my way to the central office, record my early day out from work, and then drive over to the hotel. When I get there, I move through the lobby to the elevator and then up to the second floor. Within minutes I am at the door knocking.

Tonya opens the hotel room door and takes my hand to pull me inside. After closing the door, she tells me, "We have maybe ten minutes."

"Ten minutes?" I say with a chuckle. "This is an expensive place to get a room for just ten minutes of sex, Tonya."

She shakes her head. "*We* aren't having sex, Russ." The proclamation causes my heart to sink as I hear the news.

"Wait, I thought you said..."

"I asked you to meet me here, Russ. I didn't say anything about sex between the two of us." I suddenly realize that my wife is wearing almost nothing as she stands in front of me.

"Wait a minute. What's going on, Tonya?"

Her blue eyes look hard at me. "You wanted to know what sex with Marcus was like, right? You asked me about that last night. So, I'm going to let you see what it was like, Russ. Just don't hate me too much, alright?"

"What do you mean?"

Swallowing hard first, my wife tells me, "Marcus came by my office today and we had a long talk. He is willing to let things go, but only if we have one last time together."

I gasp. "Are you telling me that you are going to have sex with him in a few minutes?"

"Yeah, I guess that's what I'm saying, Russ. The thing is, I don't think he will want you here. But, I want you to see us together." Tonya looks at the door to the room. "He will be here soon, so what do you say? Do you want to hide and watch?"

"Watch?" My cock becomes completely hard as I consider the offer. To get to see Marcus screwing my wife is something I have wanted but have been afraid to ask my wife for. Apparently she wants it too, which is why she has called me to this hotel room.

"He paid for the room right after he came by work this morning and told me that he would be here by eleven. It's nearly eleven." Tonya motions toward a door. "This is a closet, Russ. The louvered door should give you a good view of us together."

"Fuck," I mutter quietly. "Are you serious? Do you really want to do this?"

My wife nods her head slowly. "I want to do it. Are you okay with this, Russ?" She watches me intently as I nod my head as well. "Then get into the closet and keep quiet, okay? I don't want him to know that you are here or he might not do what he wants to do." Tonya pushes me toward the closet. I get inside and sit down on a small stool before she closes the door.

Looking down at my watch I can see that there are about two minutes until the other man is supposed to arrive. Putting my hands on the walls on either side of me, I steady myself as I think about what is about to happen. Never before have I seen Tonya have sex with anyone else. Up until I discovered that she was texting with Marcus, we had not spoken about sex with other peopl either. This is so different than anything I have experienced with Tonya before and I have no idea what to expect now.

A knock comes from the hotel room door. Tonya goes to the door and answers it. "Hello, Marcus," she says as her voice quakes.

"Tonya." The strong, masculine voice is firm and deliberate before the sound of kissing becomes apparent. She was right; he is not the sort of man who wastes time asking permission.

They move into view as they walk back to the bed. Marcus is tall and handsome, his olive complexion and dark hair harkening to an ancestry that appears to be Mediterranean or even Italian. They continue to embrace and kiss each other for a moment before he suddenly turns Tonya around and pushes her down over the bed.

"Marcus," Tonya whimpers as he pulls down her panties quickly. "Slow down."

"Not my style," he grunts as he drops his pants to reveal his large penis. He runs it along her wet valley and along her asshole several times as he moans. Marcus yearns for my wife and plans to have her, no matter what she says or does.

The other man suddenly pushes his johnson into my wife's tight pussy. "Oh, Marcus..." Tonya's face turns red as she stretches to accommodate his large member. He thrusts as far into her as he can, causing her small body to buck a little as he finds her cervix.

"There it is," he groans before pulling back and thrusting again. I watch as his balls squish up against Tonya's soft muff. She whimpers as he hits his stride and begins to thrust a little faster. "I have missed your pussy," he growls as he bends down and bites at her ear.

"I've missed your dick," my wife tells him as her little body is rocked back and forth with each powerful thrust. Their two bodies begin to move together as Tonya turns her head and kisses her lover. Her eyes drift for a moment toward the closet door where I am hiding and I smile. She wants me to see her getting fucked like this by her former boyfriend.

"Oh, fuck, baby," Marcus says as he pulls on her hips. He moves his hips around as he enjoys the feeling of my wife's soft vagina squeezing the sides of his pecker. The man with my wife appears to be the type who enjoys a woman like a fine cigar. Marcus is simply enjoying a sample of her before he consumes my wife.

He pulls out of her suddenly and Tonya sits up as if she knows what to do. While sitting on the end of the bed, she takes his cock, still fresh with her pussy juices, and begins to suck on it. I pre-come as I watch my wife allow the young man to push the end of it all the way to the back of her throat, gagging her occasionally as he does.

"Take it all," he grunts as he puts a hand on the back of her head. Tonya gags and struggles as Marcus enjoys his cock inside her mouth. He wants to fuck her throat and he does not allow her to stop him. There have been so many times when I have asked my wife to deepthroat me and she has refused. Maybe asking her was not the best route to take?

"ACK!" He backs out of Tonya's mouth as she nearly vomits. "It's been a while, Marcus. Be careful with me."

"The husband," he chuckles. "I guess you don't get freaky with him like you did with me?" He smiles down at Tonya as he runs his fingers through her hair.

"He's a good man," she replies. "He doesn't want to do anything that would make me uncomfortable."

He laughs. "Are you uncomfortable right now, Tonya? Do you want me to stop?"

My wife's eyes again turn toward the closet door before she answers, "I don't want you to stop right now, Marcus."

"Good." He picks up her legs and ankles, causing Tonya to fall back on the bed. He then buries his face into my wife's waxed pecan and begins to devour her nibblet.

"Oh, fuck!" She begins to grind into his face hard as he goes after her wet muffin. "Marcus, shit, you're killing me." Tonya plays with her nipples as she enjoys the sensation of his tongue and mouth on her pussy.

He looks up at her for a moment and says, "You need a good licking out, Tonya. You taste sweet and ready for me." Marcus then goes back down on her and continues to enjoy my wife's moist pie.

"Fuck, I can't..." Tonya breathes hard a few times before squealing, *"I can't...UHHHH...OHHHH!!!"* She comes hard as her lover continues to enjoy her sweet pussy juices. *"NAHHHH!!! FUCK!!! FUCK!!!"* The bed shakes as my wife's little body grinds hard into it. The orgasm overtakes her in a way that I have not seen with her before, making me glad that she is having sex with her former partner.

Tonya has yet to stop coming when Marcus gets up and pushes her legs back. He pushes his cock into her and finds her cervix, causing her to squeal again. "I want to come inside you, baby. I can't wait to come inside you." He begins to thrust in and out of her harder now than before, her toes pointing hard as he holds her ankles tightly. "You are so fucking tight, baby."

"Oh..." My wife winces as he pierces her deeply inside her womb. "Fuck, Marcus, you are so long. Shit..."

"I'm coming," he says suddenly as he pushes her legs all the way back. *"Mmmmm!!!"* His face turns deep red as he releases his seed into my wife's pussy. *"Uhhh...uhhh...ohhh...uhhh...ohhh..."* Each spurt must be powerful as Marcus fills Tonya's tight cunt with his white soup. Some of it begins to ooze out from around his cock. There is a steady stream of his jism running from her pussy to her asshole as my wife can hold no more.

As they finish, Marcus pulls out of Tonya and then rolls over onto his back. My wife drops her legs and says to him, "That was so intense." She giggles before looking over at him.

"You are a nice lay, baby," he tells her before turning to face her. They kiss a moment or so before he pulls away from her. "This could be a weekly thing if you want, Tonya."

My wife shakes her head. "I think this needs to be the end of it, Marcus. You and I agreed that we needed to stop this before our spouses found out. We can't do this again."

He sighs. "I know, but it's so much harder now that I have done this with you again, baby. You are a much better fuck than my wife."

"That's what you say to all the girls, huh?" They both laugh as Tonya puts a hand on his cheek. It reminds me of the way she sometimes caresses mine, which makes me jealous for a moment, but then I remember that they have just engaged in a very intimate act together. Of course she is going to touch him that way.

"We have to be finished. I love my husband and you love your wife, right? Besides, you have a little girl too, Marcus. You have to settle down and move on now."

He sits up and nods his head. "Yeah, I guess you're right. I do need to grow up a little." Marcus kisses Tonya on the forehead after she sits up, the semen in her pussy draining more quickly now.

"It was fun, though, wasn't it?"

"Yeah, it was fun." The other man gets up and finds his clothes. After putting them on, he leaves the room and Tonya comes to the closet door. She opens it and then backs away.

"You smell like sex," I remark as I get a whiff of the air around us.

"Really? I wonder why." Tonya giggles as she puts a hand on my face. "It's over, okay? I've had my fling." She turns to go to the bathroom, but I grab her wrist and pull her to the bed. After I turn her around and push her to the bed, she asks, "What the hell, Russ?"

"It's my fucking turn." I drop my pants and then push my cock against her soiled pussy. Pushing into her wet hole, I ram my cock in until I find her cervix."

"He came inside me, Russ," Tonya moans.

"I know," I say as I move faster and faster. My wife's body suddenly tenses as she grips the covers hard.

"AHHHH!!!" She orgasms again as I feel my own jism reaching the end of my cock. *"RUSS!!!"*

"OHHH!!!" The first spurt is hard as I come inside her sloppy snapper. *"Fuck! FUCK!!! NAHHH!!! UHHHH!!!"* I do not care that another man's semen is surrounding my cock as I put more white sauce into my wife. It actually turns me on to fuck Tonya again after Marcus finished with her. *How is this for spontaneous? Do you like this, my love?* I do not say this out loud for my wife to hear, but it repeats like a mantra inside my head.

After I finish inside my wife, I pull out of Tonya and go to the bathroom. I want to get the other guy's spunk off my dick as soon as I can. "That was messy," I laugh as I walk back out of the bathroom.

"Russ, what was that all about?" Tonya laughs as she looks down at her pussy. There is a large amount of jism running out of her now.

"That was me claiming my wife, my dear," I say with a laugh. "You are mine and no one else's. Marcus or no Marcus, I will fuck you hard whenever I want to. Do you understand me?" I smile, though I try to sound completely dominant in the way that I deliver the statement to her.

Tonya smiles and nods her head. "I understand." We stay in the room the rest of the day, showering first and then coming back to the bed to enjoy each other's company. Whatever happened between my wife and her old boyfriend, I think I have shown her that I have what it takes to make her mine. If what has happened is not enough, I am willing to attempt to show her again later on.

Chapter Ten: An Understanding Between Lovers

I squeeze my husband's hand tightly as we walk along the sidewalk. It was his idea to take the rest of the week off and just relax with each other. That decision has given both of us the chance to talk out things and to come to an understanding about our sexual interests.

"Would you want to have sex with him again? I know you told Marcus that you wanted it to end between you, but I don't want you to feel like I am trying to keep you from enjoying sex with him."

Pulling closer to Russ, I reply, "I don't feel that way, sweetheart. I'm glad that I have made that decision. You and I can focus on other things now."

"But," my husband begins before clearing his throat, "What if I want to see you have sex with him again? I liked that, Tonya. It was a real turn-on for me."

"For me too," I agree. "But I think Marcus, as my ex-boyfriend, might be too close to me and to what you want for us. If I continued to have sex with him you might eventually become jealous. It wouldn't be such a great idea to do that." Squeezing his hand again, I point toward a women's clothing shop. We go inside and I begin to look through a few of the finer clothes hanging on the racks. "Expensive," I comment while grimacing.

"It's not *too* expensive, though," Russ says as he puts a hand on my shoulder. "Pick out whatever you want, honey. I'll pay for it." He smiles as he looks at me. The love in my husband's eyes is easy to see as I take in his expression. I am sure that he would get me anything that I wanted right now, even if it meant pulling out a credit card and going further into debt.

"I don't know that I want to buy something this expensive, though. It's not really me."

"It is you," he argues. "It was you when you were with Marcus before and it's still you. Don't let me hold you back, honey. Whatever you want to have, you should have."

"Why do I get the feeling that this is about more than just the clothes?" I reply with a chuckle.

Russ embraces me from behind and says, "I want you to have whatever you want, no matter what it is. You can have sex with anyone you want to, my love. Just let me be a part of it."

I turn to face my husband while looking around to see if anyone else in the small shop has heard what he has said. "You don't mean that, do you?"

"We need to explore," Russ says. "If we are going to ever know just what we are capable of sexually and then know what we want, we have to be open to other things. You and I can do this together, Tonya. It doesn't mean that either of us goes behind the other's back. Instead, we can take the time to discover what we want."

"Everything together?"

"Everything together," Russ confirms. "If you want to have another man in bed with you, even Marcus, I am cool with that. Just let me somehow be a part of it."

Looking around again, I ask, "What does that mean for you if another woman enters the picture?"

"Do you mean for you?" my husband jokes.

"You know what I mean," I reply. "Isn't there some part of you who wants to explore what it is like with someone besides me? Is there an old girlfriend that you would like to screw around with again?" We smile at each other as we get horny with our conversation. The valley between my legs is getting wet as I think about all the possibilities that await us if we take this next step sexually.

"There might be another woman that comes into the mix, but only if you are okay with that," he answers. "I don't know who that could be right now, but we can discover that together, right? Just you and me, kiddo." Russ likes to call me kiddo every so often, even though I am more than a month older than him. It is an affectionate term that he uses to great effect whenever he wants to get me to agree with him about something.

"Alright, then. We will see where things go, Russ. Just you and I and the people we consider for our bed."

"May I help you?" a voice says off to the side.

Startled, I turn to see an older woman who works in the shop. "Um, is this on sale?"

She looks at the price tag. "It's ninety-eight dollars, ma'am. Would you like to try it on?" The saleswoman looks from me to Russ and then back to me again. I feel my face turning red as I come to realize she must have heard at least part of our conversation.

"Try it on," Russ chuckles. "I like the way it looks."

"Okay, then," I say to the woman. "I'll try this one on." The woman nods her head, takes the blouse from the rack, and begins to walk toward the dressing room. My husband makes a strange face at me before laughing quietly. I turn to follow the saleswoman as I think about Marcus and everything about him that I enjoyed. Sure, I would like to have sex with him again, but that part of my life is over. It is now time to move on to someone else. Someone who will help my marriage to Russ to be even stronger and more exciting than it has been. My husband seems to look forward to this new chapter in our lives, and I do as well. All he had to do was to give me permission, and now that I know he wants this too it will make everything so much easier. I cannot wait to enjoy another man in my bed.

TO BE CONTINUED IN
Hotwife Ups The Ante In A High Stakes Game Of Poker

Don't miss out!

Visit the website below and you can sign up to receive emails whenever Karly Violet publishes a new book. There's no charge and no obligation.

https://books2read.com/r/B-A-GIXE-USXJB

BOOKS 2 READ

Connecting independent readers to independent writers.

Did you love *Hotwife And The Boyfriend From The Past - A Wife Watching Hotwife Romance Novel*? Then you should read *Hot Wife Shared - A Hotwife Wife Sharing Swingers Romance Novel*[1] by Karly Violet!

[2]

Would you let your wife fall back into the arms of her virile and sexually adventurous ex-boyfriend?

Russ can't believe his eyes as he stares back at his wife's phone.Naughty messages exchanged between her and her ex-boyfriend taunts his masculinity.The perplexed husband confronts Tony and demands an explanation.Why, after several years of marriage and a sexually adventurous life, does his beautiful wife feel the need to exchange explicit messages with her ex-boyfriend?And not just any ex, but one that the loyal husband feels threatened by .Tonya confesses that

---

1. https://books2read.com/u/baaAev

2. https://books2read.com/u/baaAev

she misses the sweaty non-stop bedroom action she experienced nightly with her past boyfriend. And longed for it for just one more night .Russ's immediate emotions should have confusion, anger and jealousy.But they weren'tStrangely, the thought of his wife with another man piqued his interest and aroused a hidden fantasy of his.

Can a stable marriage handle the inclusion of a wife's more experienced and passionate lover from her past?

This 60,000 word romance novel explores the Hotwife journey a couple take as they introduce a virile young ex boyfriend back into the stunning wife's life and watch as their wildest expectations are vastly exceeded

Read more at https://www.patreon.com/karlyviolet.

About the Author

Sign up to my mailing list to receive the two free epilogues for 'A Hotwife Adventure' and 'Hotwife Training' and to stay up to date on all of my latest releases! http://eepurl.com/c3ICWf Sign up to my Patreon account and receive exclusive Hotwife stories every month and sexy scenes every week! https://www.patreon.com/karlyviolet

Read more at https://www.patreon.com/karlyviolet.

About the Publisher